The Night Before HALLOWEEN

To my dad, who was born on
the night before Halloween—N.W.

For Marcus, my heart's delight—C.F.

ISBN 0-439-31615-4

12 11 10 9 8 7 6 5 4 3 2   1 2 3 4 5 6/0

Printed in the U.S.A.   24

First Scholastic printing, September 2001

The Night Before HALLOWEEN

By Natasha Wing   Illustrated by Cynthia Fisher

SCHOLASTIC INC.

New York   Toronto   London   Auckland   Sydney
Mexico City   New Delhi   Hong Kong   Buenos Aires

'Twas the night before Halloween,
and all through the house,
all the creatures were stirring,
except for the mouse.
The monsters had gathered
to plan and prepare,
for the trick-or-treaters
who soon would be there.

Mummies unraveled
and put on new wraps.
Spiders found corners
and spun silky traps.

Count Dracula grinned
and slicked back his hair.
Frankenstein's bride cried,
"I've nothing to wear!"

"Hurry up!" said a ghoul
who started to yawn.
"There's so much to do
before bedtime at dawn."
So the witches brewed up
a magical potion,
which set every monster
and goblin in motion.
They blew up balloons,
and hung streamers and lights,
and decorated till
the wee hours of night.

Meanwhile the children
were tucked snug in their beds,
while visions of candy corn
danced in their heads.

In the morn when they woke,
it was Halloween Day.

There was bobbing for apples
and rides in the hay.

There were costume parties,
and games to be played.
Cupcakes and candy and,
of course, a parade!

After dinner was served,
and the kids were done eating,
it was finally time
to go trick-or-treating!
Moms re-painted faces,
and straightened clown hats,
put wings back on fairies,
angels, and bats.

Jack-o'-lanterns were set
out on porches with care.
Their grins seemed to say,
"Knock if you dare."
Gypsies and pirates
and zombies in rags,
grabbed their bright flashlights
and trick-or-treat bags.

They walked down each lane,
avenue, and street,
rang every doorbell
and said, "Trick or treat!"

But just when the children
thought they were done,
the princess said,
"We've forgotten just one."

So they walked to the house
at the top of the hill,
which gave all the kids
a spine-tingling thrill.

They stood on the porch
and were ready to knock,
when they heard heavy footsteps,
and a turn of the lock.

When what to their
curious eyes should loom,
but a wicked old witch
holding a broom.
Her cape—how it shimmered!
Her face—oh, how scary!
Her hat was so pointy,
it frightened the fairy!

The wicked witch said,
"Welcome. We have a surprise."
And the children yelled,
"Run! It's not a disguise!"

The monsters were sad
when the kids ran away.
They wanted the children
to come in and play.

The wicked witch said,
"We can have our own fun!
Come on, little monsters,
the night's just begun!"

The monsters all cheered
as they danced with delight,
"Happy Halloween to all—
and to all a fright night!"